FIREMAN SAM
AND THE LOST LAMB

story by Diane Wilmer
illustrations by The County Studio

HEINEMANN · LONDON

It was Fireman Sam's day off.

"Ah, this is nice," said Fireman Sam. "A whole day, all to myself and such a lovely day too. What shall I do?"

Suddenly the back gate opened.

"Hello, Uncle Sam," called the twins, Sarah and James.

"Hello there, you two," said Fireman Sam. "Where are you off to with such a big basket?"

"We're going for a picnic," said James.

"Please come with us Uncle Sam," said Sarah.

"I'd love to," said Fireman Sam. "What would you like me to bring?"

"We've got sandwiches and apple juice," said Sarah.

"Well, I've got a big chocolate cake in the cupboard and a bunch of ripe bananas. I'll bring those," said Fireman Sam.

"Mmm, yes please," said James. "And have you got a rug we can sit on?"

"Yes indeed," answered Fireman Sam. "I'll just pop inside for it, then we'll head for the hills!"

As they walked up the lane a big, noisy dog ran out of a
garden, barking at them.
  "WOOF! WOOF!"

"OH!" cried Sarah. "He looks a bit fierce, Uncle Sam."

"He's all right," said Fireman Sam. "He's just looking after his house. Off you go, boy, go on, go home!"

But the dog didn't go. He wanted a walk too. He wagged his tail and followed them up the lane.

"He'll soon get fed up," said Fireman Sam. "Just ignore him and he'll go back home."

But the dog followed them all the way up the hill.

"We can't have this," said Fireman Sam. "There are lots of sheep with lambs up here. Go on now, shoo!" he cried. "Go home!"

The dog scurried back down the hill with his tail between his legs.

"Good!" said Fireman Sam. "That's better."

It was beautiful up on the hills.

Warm and still, and very quiet.

They spread their picnic out and lay down on the rug, with the sun on their faces.

"This is what I call a real treat," sighed Fireman Sam. "Lots of lovely food, warm Spring sunshine and friends to chat to; nice!"

James poured out the apple juice and Sarah passed around the sandwiches, while Fireman Sam told them stories about the adventures he'd had with Jupiter, his fire engine.

They were so busy laughing and talking they didn't notice that the dog had come back.

"WOOF! WOOF!"

He barked and started to sniff around their picnic.

"Go away," yelled James. "You can't eat our chocolate cake."

The dog started to run round in circles.

"WOOF! WOOF!"

"Hey! Stop that," cried Fireman Sam. "He'll frighten the sheep. We must grab him, quickly, before he does any damage."

But it was too late. As they jumped up the dog ran off.

"WOOF! WOOF!"

"Come on," said Fireman Sam. "We must catch him."

"Right!" cried the twins and they all ran down the hill after the dog.

Further round the hillside Trevor Evans was out for a walk.

"Tum-ti-tum. Tra-la. Tra-lee!" he sang as he strolled along in the sunshine.

"Baaa-aaah!" bleated the sheep on the hillside.

"Morning, ladies," laughed Trevor.

The sheep stared at him then trotted away, all but one who stayed right where she was.

"Baaa-aaah!" she bleated sadly.

"Now then, what's up with you?" asked Trevor.

"Baaa-aaah!" said the sheep.

Trevor went over to her. She was standing on the edge of the hillside, looking down at the bramble bushes below.

"What's worrying you?" asked Trevor and then he saw for himself.

A tiny black lamb was caught in the bushes, right on the edge of a steep drop.

"Maaa-aaah!" bleated the lamb.

"Don't move!" called Trevor. "Just stay there, while I run for help."

He hurried along the path and bumped into Fireman Sam and the twins.

"Hello there, Trevor," said Fireman Sam. "We're looking for a stray dog, have you seen one running around?"

"No, I haven't," gasped Trevor. "But will you come and help me? There's a lamb stuck in the bushes on the other side of the hill. He's halfway down and I can't reach him. I'm afraid he might fall."

Trevor led them round the hill.

"Look, he's there," he pointed.

"Maaa-aaah!" bleated the lamb.

"All right, we'll do what we can," said Fireman Sam gently. "Trevor, this is a job for Jupiter. I'll go to the Fire Station and pick her up. You try to catch that dog."

"We'll stay here and watch the lamb," said Sarah.

"Rightio," said Fireman Sam. "I won't be long."

Fireman Sam hurried down the hill to Pontypandy Fire Station and climbed into Jupiter.

"Hey!" shouted Fireman Elvis Cridlington. "What's going on Fireman Sam? It's supposed to be your day off."

"I'm going to rescue a lamb on the hillside," said Fireman Sam. "Hop in Elvis, I'll need some help."

"But I'm cooking the dinner," said Elvis, and held out a frying pan full of burnt onions.

"Just leave it for ten minutes," said Fireman Sam.

"It might spoil," moaned Elvis.

"You spoil everything Elvis, so why worry about it now?" joked Fireman Sam. "Come on, jump in, this is urgent business!"

Elvis dashed inside, switched off the cooker, took off his apron and then jumped into Jupiter.

Fireman Sam drove Jupiter up the hill to the spot where Sarah and James were waiting for him.

"Quick! Quick!" they cried.

"The lamb's slipping, the bush is beginning to give way."

Fireman Sam backed Jupiter to the edge of the hill and unwound the rope ladder.

"Right Elvis," he said. "I'm going down. Hold the ladder and guide me."

Elvis swung the rope ladder out and Fireman Sam slowly went down.

"Be careful, Uncle Sam," called Sarah.

"Don't you worry, I'm always careful," shouted Fireman Sam.

Hanging from the rope ladder, in mid-air, Fireman Sam could see the steep drop down the hill and the path far below. He couldn't reach the lamb though.

"Can you get him?" yelled the twins.

"No," shouted Fireman Sam. "I'll have to move the ladder along."

He swung the ladder round.

"Maaa-aaah!" bleated the lamb.

"There you are now," said Fireman Sam. "Stuck behind the bushes. Come on, let's take you back to your mum."

Fireman Sam reached out and gently lifted the trembling lamb out of the prickly bush.

"There we are," he said as he tucked the lamb inside his
jacket. "We'll have you safe in no time."

"O.K. Elvis!" he called. "Pull me up!"

Elvis turned the lever round and round and up came the
ladder with Fireman Sam and the lamb safely on the
end of it.

"It's a good job that bush caught him," said Elvis.

"Indeed it is," said Fireman Sam. "It's a long drop to the
bottom of that hill. Still, you're all right now, aren't you?"

"Maaa-aaah!" bleated the lamb.

"Come on, let's find your mum," said Fireman Sam.

They looked up and down the hill but the mother sheep
had gone.

"I think that dog must've scared her away," said James.

"Well, we've got to find her," said Fireman Sam. "Elvis, you take Jupiter back to the Fire Station and we'll look for the sheep."

"Right-oh, Fireman Sam," said Elvis and set off back to Pontypandy.

As Elvis drove off Trevor turned up, with the dog.

"I found him running about down the hill," said Trevor. "But I managed to grab him, and I tied my belt to his collar. I just hope my trousers will stay up! Did you find the lost lamb, Sam?"

"Yes, he's here, inside my jacket," said Fireman Sam. "But now we've lost the mother. Goodness, what a day it's been!"

"Most of the sheep are over that way," said Trevor nodding to the next hill. "Try there, you may be lucky."

"Maa-aaah!" bleated the lamb weakly.

"What will you do with the dog, Trevor?" asked Sarah.

"I'm going to take him back to his house and tell his owner he must be kept in the garden from now on. See you later, Sam," called Trevor and set off down the path, clutching his trousers with one hand and his belt with the other!

The sheep stared as Fireman Sam, James and Sarah, walked up the hill.

"Baaa-aaah!" they bleated and bounded off.

"Where can the mother be?" said James.

"Look, there's a sheep over there," cried Sarah. "She didn't run off with the others, so maybe she's the mother?"

"The lamb will know," said Fireman Sam. "Let's see what he does."

He gently put the lamb down. "Go on," he said. "Go and find your mum."

The little lamb wobbled about and bleated. "Maaa-maah!"

When the sheep heard the bleating she ran straight to the lamb.

"Baaa-baaa!" she bleated happily.

The lamb cuddled close to the sheep's side.

"That's his mum, all right," said Fireman Sam.

They watched the lamb follow his mother up the hillside.
When they reached the top all the other sheep started to
bleat.

"Baaa-aaah! Maaa-aaah!"

"There," said Fireman Sam. "Now everybody's happy!"

"Can we finish our picnic now, Uncle Sam?" asked James.
"I'm starving!"

They walked back round the hill to where they'd left their
picnic, but found a flock of starlings had eaten their
sandwiches.

"SHOO!" said Fireman Sam and the birds flew off with the
crusts in their beaks.

"Well, at least we've got the chocolate cake," laughed
Fireman Sam, lifting it out of his bag. He cut the cake into
huge slices.

"There you are," he yawned. "Just help yourself."

"Mmmm, it's lovely Uncle Sam," said the twins.

"Wouldn't you like a piece yourself?"

But Fireman Sam wasn't listening. He was lying flat on
his back with the sun on his face.

"Z-Z-Z-Z-Z-Z-Z-Z!" snored Fireman Sam and James started to giggle.

"Shshshsh!" hissed Sarah. "Let him sleep, it *is* his day off."

"Yes," said James. "And what a day it's been!"

"Baaa-aaah!" bleated the sheep from far away. They'd had quite a day too!

FIREMAN SAM SAYS

follow the Country Code: always keep your dog on a lead when there are farm animals about.

William Heinemann Ltd
Michelin House
81 Fulham Road
London SW3 6RB

LONDON MELBOURNE AUCKLAND

First published 1988 by William Heinemann
Reprinted 1988
Fireman Sam © 1985 Prism Art & Design Ltd
Text © 1988 William Heinemann Ltd
Illustrations © 1988 William Heinemann Ltd
All rights reserved

Based on the animation series produced by Bumper Films
for SC4 – Channel 4 Wales – and Prism Art & Design Ltd

Original idea by Dave Gingell and Dave Jones, assisted
by Mike Young

Characters created by Rob Lee

ISBN   434 97292 4 (hb) 434 97290 8 (pb)

·Printed in Great Britain by
Springbourne Press Ltd